Chris got home after losing another patient - little did he know he was about to lose everything else he ever cared for...

Chapter 1

After losing another patient Chris headed out to clear his head, he decided to take a walk along the beach, the sun was setting over the calm blue sea as he hears loud splashing and a cry for help. He looks up and sees a woman out in the sea, struggling to stay afloat, not ready to have someone else die on his watch Chris leapt up from the sand and sprinted into the water and grabbed the woman by the arm and threw her over his shoulder, now carrying double the weight he swam back struggling to stay afloat himself.

When Chris got back to the shore he laid the woman down on the sand, and checked her pulse... there was nothing, she wasn't breathing. Instinctively Chris started to perform CPR.

After 10 minutes of CPR she finally comes to, coughing up all the water as she tries to sit up "Stay there" Chris said

"We've gotta get out of here" replied the woman coughing up more sea water.

"No, just stay there, I'll get you to safety soon" Chris assured her

"zombies" she replied before she passed out. Chris heard a noise behind and turned around to be met by a group of what must have been the living dead. All covered in blood, and with chunks of flesh missing from their skinny torsos.

"holy shit" Chris shouted picking up the woman and sprinting off into the distance with her slumped over his shoulder.

When he could no longer see the zombies Chris laid the woman back on the floor and checked her vitals again, she was alive still, just unconscious. Chris got some water from the sea and chucked it in her face to wake her up. She came back instantly.

"what the fucks going on?!" asked Chris.

"zombies -" she responds before passing out again.

Chris proceeded to wake her up again.

"When did this start?" he asked.

"in the morning" she responded coughing up more water.

"right I'm going to take you back to my place, we can talk more then," he told her "can you walk," he asked

"yes" she responded stumbling to her feet

"what's your name," Chris asked

"Olivia" she responded

"I'm Chris," He said putting her arm around him to help her walk "my house is only 5 minutes that way" He added pointing his pale white finger down a long stretch of beach.

"So are you a doctor or something?" asked Olivia.

"I'm a surgeon" he laughed back "seeing you out there I couldn't see another person die"

"Did you lose a patient today then?" asked Olivia.

"Yeah" said Chris.

"I'm sorry to hear that"

Chris and Olivia carried on walking down the empty beach as the sunset cast an orange shadow behind them.

Chris and Olivia reached the house and Chris opened the door and they both went inside, Chris laid Olivia down on the white couch and he sat parallel to here on a matching white arm chair. He rested his feet on a brown antique looking coffee table and said: "get some rest you're going to need it this could be the end of life as we know it."

Olivia laid there and said "thank you for saving me"

"It's my job," Chris said quietly "go to sleep and we'll see how you feel in the morning" He added getting up and locking the front door from the inside and shutting all the windows. Chris came back down with a blanket and said "you'll need to take them clothes off and let them dry or you'll be at risk of hyperthermia" Olivia covered herself with the blanket and took off her clothes and handed them to Chris. Who put them in the washing machine, and then hung them out to dry

Chapter 2

A few days had passed since Olivia had been saved and now she was feeling better than ever so Chris Approached her and said: " we need to get you some more clothes" handing her a long white Tshirt and some jeans. "There are clothes store a few blocks from here, we can go there now if you are ready"

"sure" Replied Olivia as she buttoned up the baggy jeans.

Chris grabbed his gun before he left the house and said "just in case" Olivia smiled and followed him closing the door behind her.

"let's take the car" Chris announced. unlocking his red hatchback. They both got in the car, and turned out of the drive onto the road wich was now scattered with burned out cars and dead bodies; it was hard to tell if the bodies were human or of the twice dead kind.

Olivia looked out of the window at the chaos outside of the house and was automatically shocked, the destruction that happened in a matter of days had the ability to shock anyone, but especially someone who grew up on a farm, in the middle of nowhere she wasn't used to seeing things like this... no one was.

"took me a while to get used to seeing all the bodies and zombies, killing my first one was the toughest thing-"

"What! you've killed one" shrieked Olivia.

"It was either that or die!" he explains, "and I didn't feel like dying" he chuckles.

They could see the store on the horizon, the store was smoking. "oh shit looks like it's on fire." said Chris.

"was" explained Olivia "the smoke is white so that means the fire is out, I just hope there are some clothes left that aren't burnt."

Chris speed up to 70 MPH and was at the store in no time. As they both got out of the car they could hear a groaning noise coming from the back of the store, they headed in Chris had his gun at the ready and Olivia was walking cautiously right behind him. They headed up to the second floor where they kept all the female clothes.

"right I'll keep watch while you load some stuff into the bags" Olivia obliged without hesitation she grabbed everything she could find and chucked it into the bag. She was done within a matter of minutes "wow that was the quickest I've ever seen a woman shop" Chris joked.

They started to head back to the car when they heard a groan coming from behind, they both turn around and Olivia was now face to face, with a huge zombie with a stomach bigger than it brain. The zombie lunged at Olivia, and she let out a horrifying scream. Chris instantly shot the zombie before it could bite her. The blood and brain matter from the zombie splattered over both of them. "see sometimes you gotta kill or be killed!" said Chris walking back to the car.

They both got in the car with the previously acquired clothes. Olivia looked to Chris and said "thank you, for saving me... again" she giggled as she put on her seatbelt.

"Don't worry about it" Chris responded starting the car.

As they head back to the house Chris noticed a man at the side of the road he had a shaven white head, and his body was so skinny you could see his bones. Chris pulled over and got out of the car and approached the man who was seemingly unaware that he was there. As Chris got closer to the man he noticed he had a red rose tattoo on his neck.

"you ok?" asked Chris moving closer to the man. But, as Chris got at arm's length with the man, the man grabbed Chris by the arm and through him onto the concrete ground. For a skinny guy, he had a lot of power. The man then proceeded to hit Chris repeatedly with a metal pole, hitting him in the back of the legs and across the back. Olivia jumped out of the car and sprinted over to the man and before he knew what was going on Olivia had tackled him and was now on top, oh him clawing at his face, meanwhile, Chris was standing back up and reached for his gun. He got Olivia off the man and stood the man up against the metal fence behind them and tied his hands to the fence with the belts they took from the store.

Chris grabbed the man by the throat and whispered in his ear. "Tell me everything you "

The man lets out a laugh and asks "what are you talking about"

Chris shot the man in the shin splintering his shin bone into pieces. The man let out a deafening scream of pain. Chris got back to the man's face and asked him again "tell me everything you know."

The man was now more compliant, "there's an armory 4 miles east of here at an abandoned mine - if u let me go I can take you there" he said as he started to cry "please don't ki -" Chris shot the man twice in the chest and once in the throat, the sound of the shots echoed through the streets and left a ringing in his ears. Olivia stood there in shock of what she had just seen. They both got back in the car and drove home, saying nothing about the brutal kill that just occurred.

Chapter 3

Olivia awoke in the morning still clearly shaken by what happened last night, Chris sat on the arm chair parallel to her and said "we gotta kill or be killed, so let's move on now. we need to go and find this mine, that he was talking about" Chris stood up and grabbed his car keys and headed to the door. Olivia followed. "what if it's a trap?" she asked.

"then we'll kill more people" he responded handing her a baseball bat. Olivia took the bat and said "let's hope it doesn't come to that"

The pair got into the car and headed east for 4 miles but couldn't find a mine "maybe he was lying." suggested Olivia.

"No" responded Chris "he was too confident and he responded to quick for it to have been a lie."

After another 20 minutes of searching the area they find what seems to be the entrance to a mine, so they both get out of the car, and ready their weapons, and start to head towards the entrance when Chris notices 2 armed guards both wearing full black hazmat suits and scary clown masks. "you see them clowns" Chris giggled. "Find some cover I'm going to take out these jokers" he whispered.

Chris crawled round the side of the guards remaining undetected by hiding in a bush. As the guards turn away Chris grabs one from behind and with one swift motion he slits his throat and as the other guard turns around he launches the knife into his skull killing them both instantly. Without a sound. Chris heads over and retrieves his knife and picks up both assault rifles and all the ammo he could find. He passes one to Olivia looks at her and says "our best bet is to take their clothes and mask and go inside like that so nobody spots us" Olivia agrees and they both put on the guard's clothes and hid their bodies. They then head in through the front door with the AR's strapped over their shoulder, and fingers on the trigger "remember we don't need to kill anyone" Olivia whispered.

Chris and Olivia were now inside the mine the floor was mud the walls were mud, and the entire place was illuminated by gas candles. There was one strong steel door "that's where the armory is," Chris thought to himself. As they walk further into the mine they notice the 6 guards sitting at a table eating what looks to be a really watery soup with stale bread. The guards don't notice them, so Olivia and Chris carry on walking past. Over to the room with the steel door. Olivia tries to open the door but its locked "fuck its locked" she whispers. "there must be a key around here somewhere" Chris whispers back. They start to look into the other rooms without doors on them, but there was nothing. "we can dig through the wall" suggests Olivia. "that won't work the walls are too thick" he responded. "I think one of the guards has the key, so what we will have to do is get one of the guards attention then take them out one by one till we get the key."

"as long as we don't need to kill anyone" Olivia whispers.

"as long as they don' try and kill us" Chris shot back. "So what I'm going to do is hide round this corner and make a loud bang, to hopefully attract one or 2" Chris then proceeded to hit the metal table to his left, the only problem was all the guards heard the noise and were now rapidly approaching their position. "sorry about this" Chris whispered to Olivia. He positioned his assault rifle and as the men came round the corner Chris shot at them all hitting and killing 5 of them. The final guy came round the corner and Chris shot him in the hand he instantly dropped his gun and fell to the floor in pain. Chris walked over and asked him "where's the fucking key!"

The downed man laughed and spat at Chris. Chris whipped the spit off of his face and stood on the man's wounded hand, the man let out a horrifying scream, and Chris raised his voice above his scream and shouted: "Where's the fucking key!"

"It's in my pocket" the man replied.

Chris shot the man in the head and took the key from his pocket. "fucking cunt that'll teach you to spit at me." he mutters.

"way to go for not killing anyone" Olivia laughed as she stepped over the bodies and took the key from Chris. She then proceeded to unlock the heavy steel door "a little help" she chuckled looking at Chris.

"Yes of course" he obliged. The door creaks and groans as they open it. Once they open the door they both notice that the room is no bigger than 12ft by 3 ft., but what they did notice was the array of guns, grenades and food all-round the place "we gotta take what we can and get out, they probably heard the gun shots, so if there's more they're coming" Chris informed Olivia

They both started loading up their bags with flash grenades, handguns, tinned food, and ammo. As they are about to leave Chris sees an RPG laying in the corner "oh mumma" he chants grabbing the RPG and slinging on his back along with the other guns he has taken.

"before we leave," Chris said pulling the pin on a grenade "run" He shouts as he chucks the grenade. They sprint out and the mine collapses with a loud explosion; they get in the car and speed away. "holy shit" Chris screamed. "That was a blast"

They headed back to the house unaware of the Black car following them...

Chapter 4

When Chris and Olivia got home they looked through the guns and food they managed to grab. They had a total of:

4 assault riffles

5 Uzis

6 handguns including one dessert eagle

1 RPG

a handful of grenades, stun grenades and smoke bombs

And, ammo for the lot as well as a good week or 2 worth of food. "I think its best we find somewhere else to stay, somewhere more secure, especially now that we have these guns." Chris suggests.

"ok, where should we go?" asked Olivia.

"lets just get on the road and find out" Chris replied. "But, first get all the stuff from the cupboards and fill up some suitcases, we leave nothing behind"

As they both started to pack Chris grabbed a photo out of the draw on his nightstand: the picture was of him and his late wife standing outside an amusement park. A tear hits the photo as Chris starts to cry, but as quickly as it started it had stopped, he wiped his face, folded the photo and put it in his pocket.

Chris and Olivia get to the car, both with one suitcase each and the backpacks full of the weapons. They proceeded to load up the car still completely unaware they are being watched. Chris gets in the car, starts it and leaves his house that he has owned for the last 12 years.

They started to head south towards Georgia. "where we going to stay" asked Olivia.

"dunno" groaned Chris

"have we got enough fuel for the journey?" she asked.

"I hope so" He mumbled.

They drove on in silence for half an hour before they saw a man about 6ft 3, with blond shoulder length hair, knelt in the middle of the road, holding a gun to his head.

"No!" screamed Chris leaping out of the car and tackling the man.

"what the fuck!" the man grunts. "why do you care if I kill myself" he adds.

"I can't let you do that, you have got so much to live for" he jokes.

"see exactly there's nothing in this world anymore besides the living dead and violent thugs."

Chris grabbed the mans gun, and through it to the side of the street. "I can see it in your eyes; you don't want to die." He says to the man, kneeling at his side.

"we are going down south if you want to join us" Chris added.

"sure," the man said.

They all got in the car and carried on driving. "so what's your name?" asked Olivia.

"Joseph" he responds. "I have a safe house, in Georgia, if you are looking for a new place to survive."

"sure, saves us having to look for one" Chris explains. "where is it?" he asks.

"It's the National Museum of Georgia" He answered with a slight giggle.

"Oh damn." Exploded Olivia "are all the displays still up?" she questioned.

"some are, but the majority have been stolen or destroyed before I was there."

"how many of you are there?" Chris asked.

"only me" Joseph responded. "That's why I was going to kill myself earlier."

The car was approaching a bridge when Chris noticed that the bridge was full of zombies.

"Oh shit" Chris exclaimed "is there another way round," he asked Joseph.

"no, we'll have to go through them," he said quietly.

"the car will die trying to go through all them zombies at once, so we'll have to have someone on the left and someone on the right running down the side distracting the zombies so the car can go through the middle. Any volunteers?" he asked.

To no surprise nobody volunteered for the death run down the side of the bridge. "fine then, me and Joe will run down the side and I want Olivia to drive through the middle.

The two me got out of the car and loaded the assault rifles and 2 pistols each and they began to walk towards the zombies. Olivia was driving in the middle of the two men "on three we go" coached Chris.

"Three two one, go!" shouted Chris as he ran to the side of the bridge shooting any zombies that got too close, the plan was working all the zombies were attracted to the noise of the guns and the smell of the fresh brains.

Olivia speed through the middle running over any zombie that got in the way.

Joe was shooting and sprinting all the way down the side, the zombies were unable to catch him due to his high speed.

Chris started to get surrounded when all of a sudden, he hears a car pull up next to him and shoot at all the zombies. When all the lifeless bodies hit the floor, he noticed it was Olivia and Joe in the car. "get in we can drive the rest" shouted Joe. Chris got in the car.

They only had half the bridge left to cross now, but all the zombies were gathering back to the middle "we've got no choice drive through them" screamed Chris. Olivia stepped on the gas and went straight into the hoard of zombies. The speed of the car catapulted a couple of the zombies into the river below, the rest were splattered on the window or wrapped around the wheels.

As they exit the bridge they stop the car and look back at the mess of dead zombies behind them and Olivia said: "there must have been at least a hundred of them"

Everyone silently agreed, and she carried on driving towards the museum

Chapter 5

As they approach the museum Joe noticed the car following them and said: "Who's that guy in the car following us"

"What you are talking about?" asks Chris looking behind him at the car.

"do you see it?" asked Joe

"yep" Chris answers. "We gotta turn left and go into that ally and when they follow us we ambush them."

Olivia follows his orders and parks the car in the ally way out of site from the following car. They all get into position, Joe on the roof Olivia taking cover behind the car, and Chris taking cover behind a bin.

They are stood there waiting for 20 minutes, and finally, the car turns into the ally. As the car drives past Chris and Olivia, Chris grabbed the driver's door and holds the gun to his head "Get out of the car slowly" he whispered sternly. The man was no more than 5 ft. 8 with a crooked nose and only a few teeth. He stepped out of the car with his hands up and said: "what the fuck are you doing homie? I was just trying to get through the ally"

"I'm not your homie" Chris shouted. "who sent you after us2 He demanded.

"Ay, what? no one sent me, you must be a bit loco ay"

Chris smacked him across the face with his dessert eagle.

You could hear the crack of his nose as he hit the floor Chris shouted: "Don't bullshit me!"

The man looked up with his nose broken and blood rushing down his face "Ay man I told you no one sent me"

Chris shot his gun into the air 3 times and then crammed the barrel of his gun into the man's left eye. You could hear the sizzle of his eye getting toasted by the hot barrel. The man let out a horrific scream.

"Tell me the fucking truth" Chris screamed "pressing the gun in further"

The man let out an even more horrifying scream as the blood ran down his face and splattered onto Chris's shoes.

"Ok, ok" he cried "I was sent here by `The Butcher`"

"Who's the fuck is that! and why did he send you after us?" he asked. As he removed the gun from his eye, leaving his eyeball still attached to the end of the gun. Chris pulled they eye ball off the gun and with his bare hands pulled the eyeball from his optical nerve. The man let out another scream before passing out.

Chris woke the man up and asked him again: "why did he send you"

"because you killed 6 of his men and stole a shit tone of guns homie" he mumbled.

"where is this cunt?" he groans.

"Fuck off you cunt, I'm not saying anymore" he chanted.

"Well, then you won't need this will you" Chris grabbed the guys jaw and forced his mouth open he proceeded to cut out his tongue. The man let out another horrific scream, as he starts to choke on the blood rushing into his toothless mouth.

After the man drowned to death in his own blood Chris hears a guy on a radio he said: "Estaban, did you find the pricks that did this? Over"

Chris grabbed the radio and in a soft calm voice he responded "Estaban is not speaking right now, probably not ever again" He giggled evilly. "but I don't know you but you know me, and that should be enough for you to know that I will kill you." Chris chucks the radio on the floor and shoots it twice.

Chapter 6

"They killed Estaban" The Butcher Exclaimed "oh well I never liked him anyway" He grunted, as he headed out to the moat of his castle. He lowered the drawbridge and in drove four cars all with four men in each, all wearing black hazmat suits and clown masks. One man got out; a scruffy potbellied unshaven man who went by the name of Dwayne. Dwayne had 2 tear drop tattoos under his left eye.

"just the man I wanted to see" announced The Butcher swinging his cleaver around. "those cunts killed Estaban!"

"Oh well, no one liked him anyway" responded Dwayne.

"Oh yeah nobody liked him, but you know what they did to him?"

"No, enlighten me"

"they cut out his tongue and let him drown in his own blood" He responded.

"Wow, that is some crazy shit, I mean even for us." Dwayne said sounding legitimately shocked.

They both headed inside the castle and pulled the draw bridge up behind them. "What did you get for me" shouted The Butcher.

One man came forward and handed him a list of everything they had. "don't give me a fucking list! tell me the good shit that you have."

The man hobbled back a few inches and said, "we managed to get: Medicine, weed, knives, and a gallon of fuel"

"Oh, nice job, see now that wasn't so hard now was it" Mocked The Butcher. "Now fuck off, all of you," he said continuing to wave his cleaver around.

A tall dark man emerged from behind The Butcher, his head was shaven, his arms littered with bad tattoos, he was wearing a white vest, with blue shorts. He greets The Butcher by saying "we know where they are!"

The Butcher instantly chuckles and said: "my day just keeps getting better, so, where are they?" He asks.

"that big museum in Georgia!" He responded.

"well shit, now we gotta kill them." The Butcher said with a wide smile on his face. "but not yet, I have things to deal with. Let me know if they move, thank you, Archie"

"Yes, sir" responds the man leaving instantly.

"Hey, before you leave where's your brother?" Asked The Butcher.

"He's back at the house sir"

"you don't ask the questions" Replied The Butcher in a quiet voice. "bring him here" he demands.

A few moments pass and the man returns with his brother. "you know why you're here right don't you" The Butcher said getting up close to the man's face.

"no -" "Don't even fucking talk to me" The Butcher interrupted. "you've been stealing ammo and guns haven't you" He questions

"No sir-" "Didn't you hear what I just fucking said" He Interrupted "That's strike two one more and you're out"

The man's brother pipes up and says, "ay I'm sure we can settle this"

"we sure can" Replied The Butcher swinging his cleaver down on the man's shoulder detaching it half from his body; the man let out a loud scream.

"Just admit it, that's all you gotta do" intimidated The Butcher.

"Ok, ok -"damn, that's strike three" The Butcher interrupted. swinging his cleaver down on the man's arm again completely detaching it this time. The man falls to the floor in a pool of his own blood sobbing loudly.

"Clean that up," the butcher said to Archie.

"Yes, sir" Archie responded trying to hold back his tears as his brother lays on the floor bleeding to death, beside his dismembered arm.

The Butcher wiped the blood off of his cleaver and carried on with his day as if nothing happened.

Chapter 7

As they arrived at the museum they are met by barbed wire barricades blocking the road directly to the museum. "don't worry I put them there" Joe reassured.

"How do you get your car around," asked Olivia.

"You don't" Joseph laughed back. "park it up here and we will walk the rest of the way"

"Let's just hope that no one steals it," said Chris.

"They won't I cleared out this entire area" Joe reassured them.

The group parked up right next to the museum and headed around the corner where they saw a big sign reading "Georgia National Museum" as Joe pushed on the old oak doors they creaked with age. "those doors don't seem safe, we should probably sort them out."

"yes" Joe agreed. "Let me show you around." He added, as he stated to walk forward he said: "There are only 3 accessible rooms, there is the security room where most of the cameras still work, the bathroom and the grand hall where most of the exhibitions are... well were they're gone now."

As Joes escorted them into the grand hall, they were astonished by how big the room really was, there was only one bed in the corner with a small table and a pile of clothes and food on the floor. "this is where we will all be sleeping" He announced.

"I guess we'll be getting beds or a sleeping bag?" Olivia asked.

"shit like that is a luxury now" Chris replied.

"that is true" Joe agreed "but I do have a couple sleeping bags in the next room"

They headed through the bedroom over to a small brown door with a sign above it that read "Security" "this is where you will be keeping all the weaponry you find, it will be locked, it is the only room that will be locked" Joe told them.

"It's good to have our armory right next to our bedroom" Chris acknowledged.

"Oh, there is one thing I must say" Joe announced. "the rest of the floors are of limits."

"Why?" asked Olivia.

"Zombies, too many to kill, even with all 3 of us, but down worry I have secured it very well. They won't be coming out anytime soon," said Joe.

So, they all went back to the suitcases and put all their guns in the tiny security room which only had 5 working cameras, one outside facing the front, one in the bedroom, one facing the balcony at the back of the house overlooking a river. One facing the bridge, and one on the roof.

Joe went to go and get the sleeping bags from the closet.

"what do you think is upstairs" whispered Chris.

"I hope it's just zombies Olivia whispered back. "I say we just leave it and hope we never need to find out."

"agreed" Chris mumbled.

"here you go, 2 sleeping bags for you guys, I got some pillows and duvets, if you need them," Joe said handing them a sleeping bag each.

"this is very kind of you" Olivia announced.

"it's the least I could do for the people who saved my life." He responds in a soft voice as he walks over to the balcony "this view never gets old" he informed them, as they gaze out the window to see the sun setting over the empty fields and the light danced across the river laying behind the museum.

"we should get to sleep earlier tonight we got a long day ahead of us tomorrow" announced Chris.

The others nodded their heads and went to sleep.

Joe fell asleep almost instantly. It took Chris and Olivia a little longer to get to sleep so they headed out to the balcony and started talking. "This could be a permanent home," said Olivia.

"I hope so" replied Chris "I don't like having to move round all the time, we gotta settle down here. we gotta make it zombie and human-proof. We're in this for the long haul, I ain't dying anytime soon. not if I can help it anyway."

"But what if he doesn't agree with the changes?" Olivia asked.

"Then we take over this place and kill him" Chris whispered.

"We should probably go to sleep now" Olivia chuckled.

"Good night," Chris said getting back into his sleeping bag.

"Good night Chris" Olivia smiled

Chapter 8

After seeing The Butcher brutally kill his brother Archie decided that he didn't want to receive the treatment that his brother got, so he told The Butcher about a military convoy driving through the area.

"Wow, but you know if I find out you are lying you know what is going to happen" Said The Butcher pointing his cleaver towards the blood-stained floor where Archie's brother once lied. Dead.

Archie clenched his fist and walks away in anger, he must wait for the perfect moment if he's going to do anything, or he'll end up dead like his brother.

The Butcher chuckled and gathers a group of his highest skilled me, all wearing the black hazmat suits with clown masks. They all got in one car, everyone had assault rifles and there was an RPG just in case things went south. The Butcher kept his Cleaver.

They drove down the road towards where Archie said the convoy would be, but there was nothing, so they carried on driving a little further and noticed the convoy had stopped in a field just off the side of the road. So, to remain undetected they all equipped silencers, and walked the rest of the way to them crouching.

As they got nearer to the Army Men The Butcher said: "there is 11 of them, on three we open fire." They all got into position surrounding the soldiers. "open fire" The Butcher commanded as he ran in, hitting one man with his cleaver and kicking another in the chest then he followed that with a devastating blow from his cleaver splitting his head in half. The Other men took care of the rest with them suppresses assault rifles.

The rest of the men moved in stepping over the bodies slumped on the floor. The Butcher headed to the camouflaged armored truck and looked inside, what he saw was a gold mine of medicines, guns and bottled water. "Holy shit." he explodes as he gets inside and notices how much there was. "There's at least $3 million of firepower another $2 million in medicines, and another $500,000 in bottled water." he informed everyone "we're set for life!"

"we can't load all of this into the car, we'll just drive this back!" He announced. The Butcher got into the driver seat of the armored truck, and headed back down the road that they came moving slowly as to not damage any of the good. Close behind him followed the rest of the group.

When they arrived back at the castle The Butcher drove the truck straight back in, and quickly shut up the draw bridge. "get Archie, anything he wants from the shop! He has set us for life" The Butcher ordered one of the masked men. The man nodded and left to go and get him.

The Butcher took Dwayne to the side and said, "we need to show that guy in the museum who's boss"

"agreed" Dwayne replied "he can't just kill out men and get

away with it"

Then man he sent to get Archie came back alone, and said: "I think you've gotta see this"

"Nope just tell me, I am not moving from this spot till you tell me" He smiled.

"Archie's hung himself in his room" He muttered.

"Wow and I was going to let him have anything from the shop, ANYTHING" He chuckled. "just deal with it, burn his body or something." he ordered.

The man obliged and headed back to the room where Archie hung himself and hanging there was a zombie Archie his eyes bulging out, his neck clearly snapped from the force of his weight on the rope. The man stabbed Archie in the head killing him instantly, and as he stepped into his 10ft by 10ft room he found a note that read:

"I couldn't do it anymore,

I've seen too much, I hear too much, the voices in my head they are getting louder and louder.

The Butcher killed my brother right In front of me.

He will get what he deserves.

Not from me, but the people at the museum, they will get him. I promise you that"

The man took the body outside and burned it, the smell that

filled the air was enough to make even the strongest man vomit. While the body was burning he headed to The Butcher and handed him the note. The Butcher giggled in response. "they won't kill us if we kill them first" He laughs grabbing a grenade launcher from the armory.

Chapter 9

Chris finished changing the front door to one that had steel locks and thicker wood, he then reinforced that with an arm on the side that can be raised and lowered to lock the door even more. "you've done a splendid job" Joe complemented.

"Someone came around earlier, someone called Archie, he said `The Butcher wants us dead, and they are coming for us`" Chris told him. "but we ain't running again, he wants to fight we fight. he also gave us the location of his castle -"

"Castle" Joe interrupted sounding shocked.

"Yeah, the cunts got a castle, he also gave us the disguise that his men were wearing. The same clothes that the men at the mine were wearing..."

"Oh shit, we've been killing all his men now he's pissed and wants us dead." Olivia pointed out.

"So, we've got to secure this place, search for better guns, and maybe more people, then we head to the castle and take them out before they get a chance to kill us. They have the numbers, but we have the advantage - we know they're coming."

They all grabbed assault rifles from the security room, and left through the front door. They headed around the corner to where their car was, and it was scratched to shit, and in white spray paint on the side, it read: "We're coming for you!" Chris laughed "fucking come then cunts." Olivia got into the car and turned the key "it still starts, let's go" she grinned.

"Let's just hope they haven't put a bomb under it" Chris Joked.

They drove through the barren town, and stopped at the gas station "they might still have some gas left" Chris laughed. He heads over to the pumps and checks if there is any sort of fuel left... he wasn't disappointed when he realized there wasn't any. Olivia and Joe got out of the car and headed towards the store; when they got to the window they noticed, that the store was untouched. So, they headed in. It was clear that people had been there before because of the blood on the floor "someone has been dragged through here" Chris whispered. He got onto his knees and touched the blood, it's still wet, and warm so they were here recently. They follow the blood trail which leads down to the basement. "oh, shit this is cliché ain't it" laughed Olivia. They opened the basement door and heard zombies, and silenced gunfire. "There are people down there," Chris said.

"Help!" a voice from the basement called.

"Go in guns blazing" Chris ordered.

They ran down the stairs and opened fire on the zombies, and within a matter of seconds all the zombies were dead.. or so they thought. One zombie came out from behind a stack of boxes and bit Joe on the fore arm. He let out a scream of agonizing pain. Olivia stabbed the zombie in the head.

"Holy fuck" Joe moaned. "don't let me die he begged"

"Don't worry we're going to cut it off?" Chris told him. "you pass me that machete" he pointed at one of the survivors from the basement. The survivor handed him the machete. Chris took off his belt and wrapped it round Joes left arm just above his elbow. "this will hurt a lot" he warned him " so bite on this" he said putting a rag in his mouth. He swung the machete down once, twice, as he hit the bone Joe let out a muffled scream. "were almost there shut the fuck up" he shouted as he swung down on his arm one last time cutting his arm off. Joe passed out instantly from blood loss.

The two survivors helped carry Joe to the car, they all got in and drove back to the museum. Where they got a hot iron, and cauterized the wound. They then laid him on his side with a drip hung from the curtain pole in the bedroom.

Chris stood up and whipped the blood from his face. "thank you, guys, for your help, you're more than welcome to stay with us; providing you have information that will help us out."

"what do you want to know" asked the smaller of the two.

"well, first, let's start with names"

"I'm Joshua," said a 6ft black man that was built like a tank with a buzzcut and an anchor tattoo on his left hand "I've served in the military as a sniper for the last 14 years" "and, you who the fuck are you?" Chris asked looking at the small white skinny kid.

"I am Alexander" he replied "I also am a military sniper"

"So as military personal you should know if there is anything going on in the area, and military presence," Olivia said.

"there was a convoy with a lot of guns medicine and food heading through, but we have had reports of it being intercepted, by someone called `The Butcher.` he took everything." said Joshua.

"Ok, do you know anything else about `The Butcher`?" asked Olivia.

"Yeah, he's going to attack this place, so you need us to help you" Alexander smiled. "we have snipers so when they do attack, we can get into position and take them out from distance."

"I give the orders" Chris shouted. "But, that's a good idea" he laughed.

Chapter 10

The Butcher enters a back room, which has a sign stating that the room is the "slaughter room." Behind him follow 2 guys both wearing the normal clothes a black hazmat suit and a clown mask. "so, I've got a mission that I'll need your help with" states The Butcher. "we're going to go steak out Chris and all of his friends"

"whose Chris?" asked the taller of the two.

"that cunt that killed Estaban" He informs him. "We set out in 5" He added, as he loaded an AK47, and put a grenade in his pocket. The Butcher climbed into the car the other 2 shortly joined him.

They start the engine and set off for a long drive from South Carolina to Georgia. The car had been upgraded to have a bigger engine, and a steel has been welded to the front in a point, to make it easier getting through crowds of zombies. The windows were bullet proof. The upgrades also made the car go faster. The Butcher was hitting 90 MPH.

He got to Georgia within an hour, and as they headed towards the bridge they noticed that the bridge was full of zombies "hold on" The Butcher said as he sped up, and ploughs through the zombies with ease.

The Butcher spots the museum in the distance "there's the museum, we'll go and stake it out from the room tops, I'll go on that one, and you two split up one of you the bridge and the other on top of the house next to it. Just don't get spotted" He demanded.

"Radio me if you see anything" He smiled.

They stand outside on the roofs for nearly an hour when The Butcher's radio goes off "there's a man out the back here, looks like he's putting down some barbed wire barriers, should I apprehend him?" asked the guy by the bridge.

"Don't move, I'll get him" replied The Butcher climbing off the roof "everyone meet me by the car - make sure you're not being followed" The Butcher demanded. In only a few minutes everyone was at the car. "Right we're going to kidnap him and find out what they know about us," he said. "we will cover his face and bring him to the car and then we will drive him to the castle."

They all moved from the car The Butcher headed round the right side and the other two headed round the left side. He waited for the perfect moment to pounce, as Joe looked away. Walked out and grabbed him from behind and put him in a choke hold, as his lungs lose air his hands curl up and his body becomes heavy and lifeless.

They carry his lifeless body to the car and cover his face, and tie his one hand behind his to his legs, and take his gun from his pocket.

They go back as fast as they came, little did they know they have left a trail of skid marks back to the castle.

As they arrive at the castle Joe is starting to regain consciousness. They take him to the "slaughter room" and tie him to a chair. As he regained consciousness he shouts "who the fuck are you"

"I'm the butcher, and you're in my slaughter room." He smiled as he got his cleaver from the table next to him. "Now you're going to tell me everything you know about us, and your friends, or I will send you back to your friends' piece by piece starting with your penis and ending with your head." He laughs.

"I ain't telling you shit" Joe shouted.

"Wow, someone wants a sex change- but you know what I'll give you the benefit of the doubt, you've got one more chance or you lose your other arm"

"fuck you" he screamed spitting at him.

"I warned you" The Butcher tutted. As he gets ready to swing on Joe's hand.

"Do it you fucking cunt, we're going to kill you anyway." He laughed

"Well shit, you gave me permission" He chuckled as he swung the cleaver onto his knuckles chopping his fingers off. Joe let out a loud scream as his fingers hit the floor, and the blood shot out splattering The Butchers apron.

"now if you tell me what you want to know, I'll stop you bleeding to death" he smiled.

"fuck you, just kill me" Joe demanded.

"that would be too easy" mocked The Butcher, as he grabbed a set of bloody pliers. "your friend Chris cut out my man's tongue... and another man's eye- that's where I start with you" He whispered getting face to face with Joe.

As Joe continues to bleed profusely he fades in and out of consciousness, so The Butcher calls in the doctor to fix Joe's fingers and wake him up.

"Rise and shine" The Butcher laughed as Joe regained consciousness. "I just saved your life; now you owe me," He tells him. "what do you know about us? about me?"

"Everything" Joe responds "you robbed a military convoy, you watched us as we crossed the bridge, and you're a cunt" He laughed

"Oh, now that's not a nice way to talk to someone who saved your life" He mocked. Joe spat at The Butcher, the spit landed on his shoe. "That was a big mistake," The Butcher said as he approaches Joe, "you're going to die today" He laughs "slowly and painfully." He adds.

The Butcher proceeds to punch Joe in the face knocking out two of his teeth, and again knocking out more teeth. He then opens his mouth and pulls out one of his teeth with the pliers. Joe let out a muffled scream, as blood starts to rush into his mouth he spits it out and mutters "you're going to die... they're going to kill you" He laughed

"You ready to die?" The Butcher asked with a grin on his face. He readied the cleaver and swung at Joe's head but he moved and only lost his right ear. "wow holy shit, your ear just came clean off" The Butcher laughed. "Dwayne" shouted The Butcher. And, in he walked, "can you take Joe's ear and deliver it to them cunts in the museum?" he asked handing him the severed ear. "put a note on it saying:

"A gift from your local Butcher, bring me, Chris, alone and your man will live, every day that he is not here, will be another body part next will be his eye then, his crown jewels" He laughed "then his head, you have three days"

The Butcher put tape over Joe's mouth and left the room leaving him tied to the chair.

No matter how much Joe tried he couldn't get free. So, he sat there waiting for his inevitable death.

Chapter 11

"Chris" Joshua shouted, as he walked in carrying a small box that was left on the door step.

"What's up?" Chris asked.

"Look inside the box." He ordered him.

Chris took the box and opened it and inside lay Joe's ear. "shit!" Chris shouted throwing the box on the floor. He held the note and read it out:

"A gift from your local Butcher, bring me, Chris, alone and your man will live, every day that he is not here, will be another body part next will be his eye then, his crown jewels, then his head, you have three days"

Chris threw the note on the floor and ran his hands through his hair in anger.

"What's the course of action," asked Joshua. By this time everyone was gathered round waiting for his response.

"We go in quietly retrieve him and leave" He answered. "I want you and Alex on the roof just as over watch just in case this goes south. Me and Olivia will go in quietly. Hopefully, while we are in there we can kill The Butcher." He joked. "we go at night and me and Olivia will wear their clothes to try and blend in."

Chris goes to the security room and takes and assault rifle and an Uzi and equips a silencer to both of them. He then hands the RPG to Alex. "Only if you really must, then you can use this"

They start loading everything into the car "we don't leave for another hour" Chris commanded.

Chris fills his back pack with flash bangs, grenades and smoke grenades. And then got into the car. "It's an hour drive" Chris announced "If we leave now it should be pitch black when we get there"

Everyone gets into the car and Chris started the engine and begins to drive across the now zombie- free bridge. "When we get there you two go on the roof and provide over watch, and me and Olivia will go in through the front door hopefully no one will question us."

"Do you not think that's a bit risky?" asked Alex.

"It will be riskier getting caught sneaking around." He answered, "everything we do now has a risk!"

After another 20 minutes of fast driving through the empty roads. They reached the castle. "Right so I want both of you to split up and go onto separate roofs and keep over watch. Me and Olivia are going to go in now" He said as he put on the clown mask.

"Good luck" Alex wished as he headed up the fire exit of an old factory.

"This is it," Olivia said as she got her assault rifle at the ready.

"We've got this" Chris laughed. They both walked in through the front gate where there were 12 men all standing around talking about nothing interesting, they managed to walk past without anyone being suspicious of them. They head in through the drawbridge, and they looked at each other. Chris whispered: "You look over there" pointing to the right side. "And, I'll look over there," He said pointing to the left side.

As they split up Chris hears a moan coming from the "slaughter room" He goes to enter when he hears The Butcher say, "I was going to give them 3 days, but oh well." followed by the swing of his cleaver and the crunch of bones breaking. He held in his anger, so that he didn't look too suspicious. He headed round to a window on the other side of the slaughter room; he looked through the window and saw the skin headed Butcher his face and head littered with tattoos and he was wearing a white butchers apron that was splattered with blood, most likely human. And, in front of The Butcher, on a cast iron table lays the remains of Joe. Just his body. Without a head. The blood was still flowing out of where his head used to be, and splashing onto the floor leaving a large puddle. His body was still spasming as it entered rigor mortis. Again Chris holds in his anger, and waits for The Butcher to come a little closer to the window before he bothered to try and kill him "I don't want to end up like Joe" He thought to himself "so I'll wait for the right opportunity."

Little to Chris's knowledge there was a man heading towards

him. The man saw Chris and instantly grabbed him and exclaimed "what the -" Chris unloaded 7 rounds into the guy's chest without hesitation.

The Butcher heard the shots and looked around, and spotted Chris. Chris started to shoot at The Butcher, missing every shot. The Butcher ran out of the room and took cover behind the door and set off a loud alarm. Within a couple of seconds, the place was covered with armed men all wearing the same clothes and mask as Chris. So, he walked past everyone hoping that he is not noticed.

As he gets to the entrance he notices that Olivia is standing there waiting for him, but before he left he let out his anger by spraying his entire mag into the guards standing at the gate. He then headed back to the car and drove back to the museum.

"He's dead ain't he?" asked Olivia.

"Yeah" responded Chris taking off his disguise. "Did you guys see anything on the roof that could help us?"

"That's a negative" replied Joshua. "But if I may ask, help us for what?"

"We're going to war with them." Announced Chris.

Chapter 12

"We were attacked last night! And, they got away!"
Screamed The Butcher to a group of 20 masked soldiers,
"they were wearing your masks and clothes" He added.
"That cunt Archie told them everything about us! So, we
attack, we go big. And, we go loud!" He chants as he starts
to pace up and down in front of the men. "We attack
tonight!" He announced. "We'll finish this once and for all"
He laughs as he dismisses the men.

The Butcher and Dwayne headed to the armory and chose
their firearms of choice "There's only four of them" Dwayne
laughs.

"Do you think this is funny?" The Butcher said turning to
Dwayne and resting his cleaver on his chest.

"No, no not at all" He responded.

"I'm not above killing you for just pissing me off" laughed
The Butcher as he grabbed a grenade launcher and loaded
an Assault rifle.

The Butcher walked away with their chosen weapons and
loaded them into the armored military truck.

The Butcher headed back to the armory, and as he grabbed
the door handle he heard someone scream: "No, stop
please" He opened the door slowly and noticed Dwayne
forcing himself onto a naked woman. "well what in the fuck
is going on here" The Butcher screamed.

"It's not what it looked like" Replied the also naked Dwayne.

"Really, because it looked to me that you were trying to rape this woman - now I don't like rapists." He informed him.

The woman sobbed in the background. "yes, he was."

"Now you're too valuable for me to kill so instead -" He swung his cleaver down on Dwayne's erect penis, cutting it off. Dwayne hit the floor and laid next to his dismembered penis. He vomited in between screams of pain. His tears rolled down his cheek and landed in the pool of blood.

The woman now sitting there still crying and shaking. "thank you" she mutters.

"Don't worry about it" The Butcher responded. "He won't be doing that to anyone else ever again." Laughed The Butcher.

The Butcher called in the doctor, as the doctor entered he said: "fucking hell, do you want me to reattach it?" He asked.

"No, don't re-attach it." He smiled

"Yes sir," responded the doctor, as he got to work.

The Butcher approached the woman and sat next to her "you don't have to worry about him anymore" He said reassuringly. "So, go have a bath, get some clean clothes, and go and get something from the store. Anything, completely free." He offers.

"Thank you, so much" She responds putting her clothes back

on. As the woman leaves The Butcher said: "Make sure he's able to go to war tonight" The Butcher then got up and left the room, seemingly with no remorse.

As the doctor works on Dwayne, The Butcher carries on loading up the truck with assault rifles, SMGs and snipers. He turned around to see Dwayne limping out, with the support of the doctor. The Butcher laughed, "Midget dick, let's roll"

They all climbed into the truck, The Butcher driving, Dwayne next to him in the passenger seat. And, they headed out of the front gate towards the museum.

Chapter 13

"We are here to remember the life of Joseph," Chris said as he started to tear up "His life taken from us by the hands of The Butcher. You will be missed by friends and family. We didn't know you long but, I considered you family" He added as he looked down at the wooded cross planted firmly in the grass behind the museum.

As it started to rain, everyone headed inside, Chris and Olivia brought to tears by the devastating death that they witnessed.

"If only we got there sooner" Chris cried.

"We'll avenge him today; The Butcher will get his comeuppance" Joshua comforted him.

They sat in the bedroom, the only sound was the sound of the rain hitting the window, as well as the occasional clap of thunder, accompanied by a flash of lightning. "Today we end all of this" Chris said, fighting back the tears. "We will avenge Joe and we will move on."

He got no response from anyone. "we've gotta leave now -" He was interrupted by a loud truck horn.

"Shit, they're here." Chris whispered. "Alex get to the roof with a sniper, me, Olivia and Joshua will take care of the people on the ground."

Olivia locked the front door, and lowered the arm to give

them some time. Chris gave her a high-powered assault rifle, with a scope. He then handed Joshua two mini Uzis, both with laser sights. "Good luck guys," Chris said as he headed to a window and opened fire at the men, his bullets ricocheted off the armored truck. The men dove for cover, and started to return fire smashing the semi-open window that Chris was shooting out of.

Olivia and Joshua got to the other windows and started laying down fire, killing four people. The Butcher stood at the back and shouted: "Come out Chris and we'll let your people live, or stay in and we'll kill all of you" He laughed.

"Fuck you" Chris shouted as he chucked a frag grenade out of the window, it bounced next to the truck, all the men dove for cover. "I gave you the choice!" The Butcher shouted, as he cocked a grenade, and chucked it through Chris' window. "grenade!" Chris shouted as they all sprinted to the other side of the room. The grenade exploded creating a big hole, and blowing a hole opening up the upstairs, there were now zombies falling into the room. Chris immediately unlocked the door and ran out. He was face to face with 6 masked men, one grabbed him in a choke hold from behind, but Chris managed to bite the man's thumb off. As he bent over in pain he dropped Chris who sprayed his assault rifle killing only 3 of the men, and then out of nowhere Alex jumped down behind them, he slit one man's throat, killing him instantly. He then shoots the other two as they turn around to face him. Chris and Alex nod at each other and carry on round the right side where they are joined by Olivia and Josh.

All the zombies were emptying out of the room and dining on the unexpected masked men. The gunfire, and screams of people being eaten alive echoed the streets. They see in the distance Dwayne raise his gun up to the back of The Butchers head, but before he shoots a zombie comes out of nowhere and tried to bite him. He kills the zombie, with his knife. "Thank you" the butcher shouted.

Chris chucked a smoke grenade at The Butcher, now unable to see the zombies The Butcher and the remaining men were forced back to cover by the adjacent house. Still firing at the zombies, The Butcher and his men were unaware of Chris, Olivia and Joshua, flanking round behind him.

When they got behind The Butcher Chris grabbed him in a choke hold and shot the 3 men in front of him. The Butcher lands an elbow to Chris' ribs, Chris drops him, The Butcher stumbles to his feet. And runs off into the smoke. Chris moves up but is cut off by the remaining men, they shoot at him hitting him in the leg. Olivia and Joshua shoot at the men killing them all, they sprint to go and help Chris. When all of a sudden, the engine of the truck turns on and Dwayne presses his foot on the gas. The four-ton truck hit's Joshua pushing him under the truck, the back wheel sped over his head, squashing it, splattering his brain all over the floor.

The zombies were reaching Chris when Alex shot them and grabbed Chris by the arm and carried him to the car, they get in the car. Olivia got in the driver seat. And they drive off in the opposite direction to The Butcher. Not knowing if he is alive or dead.